Swati's Marriage
and Other Tales of India

Ankita Sharma

World Voices Series from

Modern History Press

Swati's Marriage and Other Tales of India
Copyright © 2016 by Ankita Sharma. All Rights Reserved.

From the World Voices Series

Distributed by Ingram Book Group (USA/CAN), Bertram's Books (UK/EU)

Library of Congress Cataloging-in-Publication Data

Names: Sharma, Ankita, 1984- author.
Title: Swati's marriage and other tales of India / Ankita Sharma.
Other titles: Swati's marriage.
Description: First edition. | Ann Arbor, MI : Modern History Press, 2016. |
  Series: World voices series | "Distributed by Ingram Book Group (USA/CAN),
  Bertram's Books (UK/EU)" -- Verso title page. | Description based on print
  version record and CIP data provided by publisher; resource not viewed.
Identifiers: LCCN 2016000598 (print) | LCCN 2015043575 (ebook) | ISBN
  9781615992881 (ePub, PDF) | ISBN 9781615992874 (pbk. : alk. paper) |
  ISBN
  9781615992881 (e-book)
Subjects: LCSH: Marriage--Fiction. | Families--Fiction. | India--Fiction.
Classification: LCC PR9499.2.S2573 (print) | LCC PR9499.2.S2573 A6 2016
  (ebook) | DDC 823/.92--dc23
LC record available at http://lccn.loc.gov/2016000598

Modern History Press
5145 Pontiac Trail
Ann Arbor, MI 48105
www.ModernHistoryPress.com
info@ModernHistoryPress.com

Toll free USA/CAN: 888-761-6268
Fax: 734-663-6861

Contents

The Revelation

The wind bedashed against the wide window panes, and she watched the trees swing wildly. The soft murmur of the air conditioner and the occasional beeps of the various machines from which several wires entered her veins, like the venomous tentacles of a blood-sucking beast, made her wither in discomfort. She tried to move, but the machines would just beep loudly to protest and arrest her as if she were a deadly criminal. She watched the trees and the glittery wind chime, the one she got from Switzerland, dancing happily. She closed her eyes and recalled how she would throw handfuls of snow at her husband and their never-ending sweet nothings over candlelight dinners in Interlaken at Switzerland. The joy she had experienced during her honeymoon had seeped into her blood and often made her smile when the pain was too much to bear and was made worse by the bitterness that pills and capsules spilled into her life. She closed her eyes and took a few deep breaths; then clutching her rosary tightly, murmured a small prayer. She wanted to get up all of a sudden and fold the untidy piles of clothes lying on the couch, check the kitchen groceries for stocks, arrange his wardrobe, and single out clothes that required cleaning. Her mind still wished these things, but with a body stuck inside the deadly jaws of cancer, a tear fell into her ear, making her shrug her face and silently curse her fate at her helplessness.

"And this?" A chirpy girl, in her late twenties, maybe three or four years younger than she, entered like a flash of lightning, carrying an expensive-looking wooden box with intricate carving done upon it. The girl sat beside her and opened the box with uncontrollable excitement. "This will look good only on Indian wear, you see, those ethnic suits and saris and all," said the girl, moving her manicured fingers, with nails painted in several colors, over the turquoise beads of a necklace. "No? What say?" she asked.

"And these? My God! They match perfectly with my burgundy evening dress; remember the one I got from Goa!" she added without looking at her. "You have an awesome collection; I must appreciate your choice. You have the best! The best of everything...." Her cheer faded like a morning dream and she acquired a serious bearing. She then stood in front of the full-length mirror, near the washroom, and stared, admiring her long tresses. "This, look at it," she said, pointing towards the tiny black dot above her lips, "makes people weak; they can't get enough of it," she added proudly, as if flaunting an international record. She hopped back and picked the box up; then she opened the wooded almirah, took out a square hand mirror, not very small, gave a slight kick to the flap, and sat beside the woman, too uncomfortable to speak or protest about her jewelery box, another one that was being scrutinized.

"See, you...you will manage..." the woman said slowly.

"What?" asked the girl, admiring a pair of glass bead earrings.

"I do not know if I will be..." the woman choked.

"This will go well with all my pink dresses."

"I have only one concern."

"Pink and pink...too similar, isn't it?"

"All day, it is eating into my heart."

"These days, heavy earrings are in vogue. I noticed a few heroines too wear heavy ones with Western dresses."

"I mean...he can manage himself, but an innocent heart does not understand."

"Black goes with everything! I mean, where have you managed to get these lovely pieces from?"

"An innocent mind needs love, care, and attention."

"Hmm... yes."

"A kid would want his mother even though he has everything at his service."

"Yes, I know.... Will black suit on my dusky skin tone? You fair-skinned ones can try everything, but we do not have much choice. Alas!"

"A mother, who is his guide... friend... supp.... See... my child will be left alone," she said after a moment.

"And what makes you feel like this? Wow! I mean, simply superb! Now I love a gold and maroon combination, and I know *jijaji* loves it too!" the unconcerned girl chirped, opening the lower half of the box, swinging a long necklace in her hands.

"That day, when we went to the marriage of Mr. Bhalla's daughter, he told me that he loved my get-up only because of this particular combination! These men...he is just so timid in giving compliments... sweet!" she said, grinning and then smiling shyly to herself.

"Wedding?" asked the woman, blinking to make the thin veil of water disappear.

"Oh, yes, it was last week; you had your chemotherapy thing all that day, so we forgot to tell you," replied the girl carelessly.

"Okay, leave it.... My child... what will he do without me?" the woman began to cry.

"Why the hell are you always crying? You are undergoing chemo, right? Then wait for the results, and all this death and all are matters of fate. What can anyone do in this?" The girl suddenly got up with the box and pressed a tiny bell switch that made the nurse, dozing after her lunch break, rush inside to attend her patient. "My dear, do not worry; *Jijaji* is doing whatever he can, and for God's sake, you do not forget that he also needs attention and care," she added, trying to make her tone seem softer than it really was.

"I...I want a promise from you," said the woman, gathering some energy and speaking softly.

"Yes, I am here. Do not worry," she said, trying to fix a bracelet with one hand onto another.

"I never even imagined that this would happen to me.... Oh! I was so healthy, and then one day, this cancer spread like a poison in my flesh... this cancer, this ever-throbbing devil... this...." The woman spoke intently in one gasp, but choked when a gush of tears trickled down her cheeks and made her hollow cheeks appear darker and her half-bald head like a barren desert with sand dunes all over.

"Your life has been very good. Leave all to God. He will take care." The girl threw a quick glance at her and smiled as she managed to fix the bracelet successfully. "These bracelets are difficult to wear with one hand."

The machine gave out some weird beeps, and the nurse quickly stopped chatting on her mobile and gestured the woman to stay calm, patting her thin hand that resembled a dried branch of an old tree that once was laden with fragrant flowers.

"Yeah...I am listening," the girl murmured, fiddling with a hand embroidered pendant. "This is rare!"

Suddenly, a child, not more than four or five years old, entered the room quietly with a school bag that was indeed heavy for his delicate shoulders, and a half-filled water bottle hung around his frail neck like a dead albatross. He somberly sat beside the lady and stared at her in blank silence.

"Had...lunch?" she asked him softly, to which the little boy shook his head slowly.

"Why?" she asked, but he just kept staring at her with his large curious eyes.

"Why? Why did you not have lunch, honey pie?" asked the girl, patting his head, and then took out a sari from the wardrobe, kept carefully folded under a few files. "Go, change," she said, and a middle-aged man with an apron around his wide torso came in and took the child.

"Your kid and his tantrums...oh!" the girl muttered under her breath. "I mean so cute!"

The woman stared at the black clouds forming outside, telling that the tempest was about to arrive. The wind chime made the loudest noise it could, and the furious winds tried hard to break into the window.

"Children need love and care," the woman added, staring sharply at the girl, busy in matching the sari with one of the pieces of artificial jewelery in the box.

"Yes," she said coolly. "Your real collection must be very good, right? He is really not at all a tight-fisted nerd."

After a few uncomfortable moments for the woman, and those of indulgence for the girl and indifference for the nurse, the little boy arrived and sat beside the woman. "Have your lunch, my love," the woman told him softly with much concern, but he just nodded blankly.

"See...he is not eating properly these days," she said with much worry dripping from her hollow face.

"Take lunch, kid. It is necessary. We all have our lunch on time," added the girl, folding the sari. However, the boy would not budge, making the woman somewhat depressed.

"See, he is not..." she added.

"Go and eat. Okay. Come along," added the girl, pulling him by the arm. She shouted for the manservant, who came promptly and took the child outside.

"These kids!" The girl gave a smile and sat beside the woman.

"Your sari collection rocks! Are there more? Let me put naphthalene balls into the folds; otherwise, you won't even get the hint and moths will destroy the entire wardrobe," she said, stroking the sick woman's head; touching her skin very lightly and leaning towards her, added, "I am here; I will manage."

"Moths," the woman said after a few seconds, looking the girl in the eye. "They have got in already."

"Oh! So give me the keys," said the girl, creating a sense of urgency.

"My child? Will he be all right after I am gone?" the woman asked in a mellow tone.

"Yes, I am here. You will get all right," the girl replied.

"Will you take care of him, give him love and affection till he becomes old enough to manage for himself?" asked the woman, clutching the smooth bejeweled fingers of the girl with her rough ones.

"Yes...he will be fine, I am sure," she replied with a poker face.

"I wan..." the woman began when the child hopped in and stood near them.

"Look, the little devil has come! I told you, he will be all right. The keys?" the girl said, dissolving some sweetness in her voice.

"What did you have, my dear?" asked the woman, and the child smiled in response, making the curves of her lips go up too.

"This throbbing pain..." she complained and tried to shift on her bed a bit, but the girl put her arm on her weak shoulders and said, "See, you worry for no reason. I will handle the clothes before they are destroyed, so keys please?"

"It is not so urgent," the woman replied, and she made the boy sit near her, stroking his tiny hands with hers. The girl looked at them, walked casually to the mirror, and carefully darkened her kohl a bit, and with a small brush, dabbed a little blush on her cheeks. After a moment's brooding silence, the woman called the girl and began, "After me, will you take care of his emotional needs? He is a child, all of four years.... He needs love and aff...."

Suddenly the girl, who was now sitting droopily on the chair, came to life. She jumped at the car horn and rushed towards the mirror, freshened up a bit, wore one of the earrings pair from the wooden box and the gold and maroon long necklace, and got up to rush like a dart, but suddenly stopped in her tracks and stared at the woman, looking at her acutely. She then untied her long hair and let her mane flow freely, like a tarantula's tentacles, and ran outside with much elation.

The woman choked on tears, pulled her son closer, and murmured, "Be upon yourself... do... not... expect... God.... He... is... there.... I... will... be... around... forever. I... son," and burst into tears. The boy took a folded hanky out of his pocket, after a little search. She kissed his hand frantically and said a small prayer, her chapped lips moving as dry leaves rustle on ground. Outside, the black clouds burst, spilling their wrath ferociously. Her wind chime broke and pieces scattered across the floor.

* * *

Swati's Marriage

On a creaking bed, Swati lay tired and irritated, shutting her eyes and ears tightly. Every minute or two, she would mutter something comprehensible only to herself. Her frail father, who was on heavy medications, slept in the adjoining room on a cot. Once more, she cursed the annoying wedding rituals and the music blaring outside that always flooded people with joy and elation but made her feel even more miserable. She hated weddings; she hated the rituals and the swirl it brings into one's life.

This was not a novel experience, and it sucked every drop of patience out of her tired soul; rather, every wedding exhausted her. She stretched her legs and tried to shut herself between the mattress and the cushion that seemed to cry out for repair, just like rest of the house. The chipped walls of the small room that could barely contain a few pieces of old furniture made her feel sick very often. She loathed herself; she loathed her life and its aimless existence. Every strand of motivation inside her seemed to have ruptured, and she felt weak carrying the burden of a colorless and dull life everywhere.

Only a few hours back, she had stood silently at a crowded bus stop, craning her neck once in awhile to stare at the busy main road. A few days back, she had to take an auto-rickshaw home, and since then she had tried hard not to miss her bus. People crowded the only twisted and broken iron bench on the stop, but she kept standing for more than half an hour. The never-ending honking of traffic and the strong stench of petrol and diesel filled everyone's nostrils, compelling most of the people to cover their mouths with whatever piece of cloth they found most handy. Handkerchiefs or corners of *saris* and *dupattas* had never seemed so useful. With one hand, she covered her mouth, not really to save herself from the overdose of smoke but from the urchins hanging around with their preying eyes, feasting upon anything they thought resembled a woman. Here, like all women, Swati was in genuine danger. Her thin silhouette had always attracted more attention than she had bargained for, though it had also helped her to fetch her job as a receptionist right after she graduated. This time, a relief filled her face.

The bus was on its way, and she could already see some hope of finding a seat on it. As soon as it arrived, people swarmed through the open gates like an angry mob going on a sacrilege. The noise, the hustle-bustle, made her clutch her only handbag even more tightly. Shoulders rubbed against each other; people shouted, cursed, and requested seats. Most grabbed them when they could spot one. After years of such practices, she too had gained a sort of mastery and managed to get one as soon as a burly old man stood up with his attaché case, grinning at her. She leaned against the window, feeling the cold harsh air damp with fuel, and absorbing all the suffocation inside the small elongated compartment that had started moving by then. A lady with two children, one in her lap and the other holding her arm, sat down beside her. She glanced at them, and then for a few moments, closed her eyes to cut herself off from the ever-increasing noise to relax in the warmth of her thoughts. She knew exactly when her stop would come; after all, she had been travelling the same bus and the same way nearly more than a decade. Resting her head on the rusted iron window grill, she entered her dream-world, her escape from the same rotten conditions that had confined her life for more than three decades. It was a rusted cage that made her feel trapped and servile; it made her feel helpless, like a frail bird trying very hard to break free while knowing somewhere inside her heart that to do so would be a futile attempt.

Crossing the dusty alleys filled with heaps of filth here and there, she entered her colony, a mushrooming society of small houses, close and compact like a stuffed almirah, pushed to the limits of capacity. The unpaved roads and broken streets were not new to her, and they made her pray for someone to come and take her to smoother lanes one day. Hoping and dreaming, she walked up to one such house, small but her own, where her family had moved after her father's accident, to afford his treatment.

Swati rang the bell and was greeted as usual by her mother. She too had aged beyond her years, and the bags under her eyes made her look even older. As she entered, she saw her father trying to smile at her with his sunken eyes and twisted facial muscles, which were always filled with expressions of a painful realization of a lifelong helplessness and dependency upon people while trying to pull pieces of a shattered life together somehow.

"Shweta will come late today," mother said slowly.

"Okay."

"She has joined at one more place," she hummed softly.

Swati sat under the fan, pulling forward a chair, but she could not help noticing the frayed ends of the cane coming out from the sides. *This too needs repair*, she thought and glanced at the house, its flaking paint crying for a wash and the old furniture barely managing to pull itself along. Frayed ends hurt; things must come to a logical end, and they must be in their proper place. The entire place suddenly became a huge mirror; the walls, the chairs, and the entire place seemed to reflect her weary, tired, and cracked soul. With eyes glued to the floor, she contemplated deeply till she was shaken out of her slumber.

"Gift...I have to buy a gift," said her mother. "Mr. Singh's daughter is getting married today." She continued, "Why do parents marry girls at such a young age? She is still in her mid-twenties. She should see the way the world works, right?" she asked curiously and looked at Swati, expecting a confirmation, but she received a dead silence instead.

"Girls must be working, right? Marriage is no guarantee of happiness; it can make life miserable too," her mother prodded again.

"Hmmm," Swati mumbled, unbuckling the straps of her sandals.

Mother had changed into a better *sari*, but even then, her melancholy peeped through it. Swati took her wallet and handed out a hundred rupees currency bill. Mother stared at her and then took it silently. Swati again checked the wallet and let out a silent sigh. She might have to go to the ATM the next day; this was worrying as it was only the middle of the month.

"Shweta has taken an extra tuition, and Saurabh will work overtime now; his exams are over," her mother said hopefully.

She closed her eyes and lay against the wall, exhausted, holding the empty cup of tea. She remembered how a few months back a suitor had arrived for her. The family was not that well settled, but could not be called poor. She dived deeper into her thoughts and the entire scene came up before her eyes— a memory that hovered around like a phantom, refusing to leave.

One summer afternoon when the scorched land craved relief and the trees hopelessly wilted a bit more every minute, Swati opened the suitcase and took out one of the three *sarees* worth wearing on occasions. Her mother docked her up and applied whatever the small bottles of cosmetics still had remaining in them. The eyeliner and the lipstick gave a new hope for securing a settlement in life, a shoulder she had been craving for and a love that would hide her from all the lecherous gazes and stares she had been bearing silently and the slog she loathed. Every day, she pulled herself up for a fight that would leave her alone and sad every evening, and the next day, she would again submit to her fate, reluctantly going to the same office every day.

The suitor worked in a private company as something, but looking at his indifference, she doubted his interest in marriage.

"My son is a diamond," his fat mother dressed gaudily in strange eye-pinching color combinations cheered, holding the frail boy by his drooping shoulders. "He is an M-B-A," she added with utmost stress on the last words, and then she quickly changed the topic before anyone could ask further while her son just sat there like a droopy dog, waiting for his masters to finish their business and give him food.

Even before they could talk alone for a few moments, his enormous mother made it clear that she would not allow her would-be daughter-in-law to be so generous towards her own family, especially in financial matters. The boy looked still the same— as if waiting patiently to get the thing over so that he could go home and relax properly. He rolled his eyes in impatience and discomfort, making Swati feel a bit miserable. After heartily gorging on evening snacks, they too, like many others, left promising to convey their decision.

She opened her eyes; the flickering light coming in from the open window danced on empty wall in front of her. "Dinner is almost done," her mother called from the kitchen, loud enough to make her listen amidst the noise that had now begun outside. "It seems the *baaraat* is about to come," she said as she tried to draw Swati into conversation.

"Hmm…yeah…" she replied. The mother sat beside her and, taking her hand in her palms, said, "Only a few years to go; after that, your brother will earn his post-graduation degree and will start working, and Shweta too will find someone willing to marry her without much demands," she said, wiping the corners of her eyes.

"Hmmm."

"I can understand you need security and care in your life. It has been more than a decade you have been working all day like a machine, but patience is always rewarding, dear, is it not?" she said, and continued, "After all, what is there in marrying early? Couples fight and get separated, or else women suffer silently. Look at yourself; you are independent and working; no one would be able to dominate you. Early marriage is indeed a curse," she said, trying to make things look rosy, and stood up to leave. "Take rest and have dinner," she added, tapping Swati's shoulders before she left reluctantly.

Inside her room, Swati pulled out an old alloy hand mirror from the drawer and tried to admire herself. Her maturity was beyond her years and fast sprouting grey hair reminded her of the spring of her youth that was fading like a morning dream. Her face had shriveled like a fresh and fragrant flower left in the pitiless weather to wilt and die; she tried to smile, but she could not. She put the mirror down and lay thinking about all the dreams she had harbored. Even though she knew she was not of much use without a sizable dowry, a speck of hope was still alive somewhere deep inside her lonely heart, a hope of getting love and care from a man who would steal her away to a wonderland where only laughter and not the painful moans and laments would prevail. She saw herself laughing and swinging in the breeze and running in the same garden that was set as wallpaper on her office desktop, wearing the same red dress she had seen at the bridal special sale in the corner shop, and could not help but admire it for a full ten minutes.

Suddenly, the shrill noise coming from outside jolted her up. Swati went near the window and saw a man decked in glittering blue perched upon a bony horse; the *baaraat* had arrived. The ladies done up heavily in gaudy makeup danced like possessed beings, and the gents, mostly drunk, vied to give them company. A typical band flanked by rows of bright green tube-lights played the usual hit numbers in the utmost cacophonic way.

All of a sudden, like an unexpected guest, a smile appeared on her dry lips. She fantasized about herself being in that red dress, and for a few moments, her face became relaxed and calm. Only moments later, she pulled herself back to the painful reality and shut the window tight. The noise still flowed in from the crevices. She tried hard to avoid the dreams that never left her heart—that were always there to remind her that she literally craved for a support. The noise made her feel more miserable than frustrated. Tears swelled up in her beautiful eyes. She buried her face in a cushion and lay on her side, closing her ears with her palms tightly, and muttered to herself that marriage might make life miserable too.

* * *

Birthday

I saw them often, for they used to live near my house. From the window of our first floor, I could see a good portion of the community park, built by government but taken care of by the Residents' Welfare Association. Earlier when exams would be going on, I would often sit up till late to study and revise the notes I made during the day. When I would go near the window to switch the lights off, I could clearly see their thin bodies sitting on that corner bench under the Alstonia tree, staring at something in the horizon. Many a time, when I would wake up early and the dew was still fresh on the green leaves and closed buds, I could easily guess their presence, and mostly, my guesses were true.

I have a particular liking for nights, and all those who know me beyond hellos can confidently bet that I am a nocturnal being, staying awake till late easily and not getting scared by the stark darkness and strange sounds of the night. There's nothing to be so pompous about this thing, but still, for some reason I know not, I take pride in this fact! The silent movement of the moon, in different shades of white, almost every other day between the grey-black clouds, along with the various intermingled sounds of tiny creeps from frogs, a few birds, and strange insects I have never seen, keep me company when I stay up till late to ponder over something or solve crossword puzzles.

Their house was third from ours, a single storey one in dark blue and an unkempt patch that they did not bother to beautify ever since they shifted here some two years back. Every morning, their son would go to his office in an expensive-looking black car, and his plump wife, whose fairness made her look rather like a loaf, would wave to him, raising her flabby arms and giving him her gap-toothed smile. Their two children were as chubby as the mother, and when the three walked on the narrow colony roads, they left little or even no space for other pedestrians.

That morning, I woke up early, as I would do sometimes, and went for a stroll in the park, tiptoeing my way from the stairs and opening the doors as quietly as I could. You could say I sneaked out of the house to take a comfortable walk in the early light, not yet intense enough to be referred to as day. I took a walk on the side paths made for joggers, and then after two or three rounds, entered inside, strolling on the wet and soft light green grass, dark only in patches. The Bougainvillea plant bloomed in three or four colors and climbed the chipped brown wall of a corner house. The orange and red leaves mingled together to create a lovely contrast while the white one stood at a corner calmly, as if unconcerned with all the climbing and contrast business. The trees housed many nests, and anyone willing to crane his neck a bit could see a few of them. The sun, as if it were still yawning somewhere, but only a few young rays, like an enthusiastic child who always rushes ahead of the parent, touched the earth, setting the temple bells to go crazy! I spotted them again; both sat quietly on a bench, murmuring something between them. The man must have been in his early seventies and, just like his frail wife, had pearly white hair and sagging skin. The woman must have been very striking in her spring, for her features gave testimony to this fact. She was not very tall, but could not be called short, just like her husband, who sported a light beard and kept a metal-head walking stick that looked really sturdy. For some reason, I find hard to describe in words how I was kind of drawn into their closed world, that began earlier than the sun and ended past midnight and stretched from their house to this rusty bench, under the old Alstonia tree. Silent and closed things are the most intriguing of all that we find attractive in this world. I gathered some confidence and extended a few steps towards their side, only to change my way in between and, instead, came home and slept for another two or three hours.

After a few days, when the clouds hinted rain and birds chirped more loudly than on usual days, I went again for a stroll. The park was all empty in the early hours of the morning except those two, who were also taking a stroll. It was indeed a different sight. I smiled at the old lady, who promptly smiled back. This happened for a week or so till the man asked me my name in the manner of a loving grandparent and we had a little chat. They told me about their retired life, their family and some surviving cousins living far apart and, of course, their son.

"He is Karan, our son," he said.

"Quite naughty he was, and I had a hard time managing him," the lady said with a glow in her sunken eyes.

"He works in an MNC here," the man said with a smile and told me about their native place, their transfer tales, and about their family.

"So, you did not resist?" I asked, surprised after they told me about the love marriage of their son to a girl from a different community and his plans to run away with her that he had made clear to them.

"No point; love just happens; community does not matter," the man added with a grin.

"So, is she a good daughter-in-law? I see her waving at your son every morning and sometimes waiting for him in the late evenings," I added.

"Yes," the lady said after a moment and changed the topic.

"Are you not bored with this park, this bench, and spending so much time here?" I asked out of my natural curiosity.

"Actually, the doctors tell us to take strolls and some sunlight. Also, we are early risers, and our son requests us every day to take care of ourselves. He is very serious about our walks and regular medicines," said the lady after a few minutes.

"You are lucky! Aren't you?" I said cheerfully.

"Yes," the man said in a plain tone as if just to keep the conversation flowing.

"Yes, they love us. They touch our feet the first thing in the morning, and nothing is done without our presence," the lady said to me and to another neighbor who, too, had joined us that early morning.

"*Auntijee*, you are really blessed. What did you eat when this son of yours was going to be born?" asked the neighbor, adjusting her tight track pants bursting at the seams, over her enormous bottom!

"Tell me, *Auntijee*!" she added cheerfully.

The old lady bit her lips and smiled while the man looked at his hands, stroking his clearly visible blue veins and rubbing the silver chain of what looked like a very old wristwatch, with a tiny bird printed on the deep blue dial with a poker face expression.

"Pray to Him that he will take care," she said after thinking for a few minutes, pointing a finger towards sky that was still filled in the shades of grey, light purple, and some charcoal black.

The next day, I could not sleep early and busied myself in solving the daily crossword till I noticed the window panes banging with swift winds carrying the rumor of rains. I put on a shawl and sneaked outside to the park where I saw both of them sitting on a bench, a different one this time. Out of curiosity, I walked up to them and asked, "Uncle, haven't you gone to sleep?"

"Actually, this breeze is pure, so I thought I should enjoy it," he replied with a faint smile, coughing in between.

"We rest the whole day, and it is not good to stuff yourself with rich food all the time, so walks are necessary," the woman added with a smile.

"Are you…going to sleep here?" I asked, shell-shocked after I noticed a mat and two thick shawls folded beside a water bottle and a small jute handbag.

"Actually…we need this air as one needs medicine," the man said. I could not stop noticing his sore throat.

"But you have a sore throat, Uncle. How will you manage here? Have you told your son?" I asked with utmost concern.

"Actually, Karan and Tina were adamant that we stay at home, but I was feeling a bit claustrophobic, so we decided to spend a few hours here," said the lady, interrupting hastily like a kid.

"All right. It is going to be midnight soon, and I should rush too. This water-laden zephyr can put me down with fever and cold," I said and began to get up, but then something happened that I can never forget.

As the clock hit twelve, a loud blare arose from their house, situated a stone's throw from the park. A few firecrackers burst in vibrant colors and "Happy Birthday, Tina" boomed in the silence of the dark. The sounds grew a bit louder before fading fast and chants of "Haaappppy- Birrrrthdaaay-Teeenaaa" turned into a bright chatter and sounds of hysterical laughter and celebration. I turned my gaze from the brightly lit house to two feeble beings, and it seemed suddenly we all fell short of words and a somber and strange uncomfortable silence covered us like a shroud. They looked at me helplessly, and I did not fail to notice a drop twinkling in her eyes.

* * *

A Happy Marriage

"See, try to listen first and then respond. I have a valid point here and it is serious," the daughter said with utmost earnestness spread all over her face.

"I am not getting your problem because it exists only in your idiotic mind. Young girls like you do not understand what value a stable and good married life has." The mother drew a long face to indicate clearly that her patience was being tested.

"No, Mummy, but please talk to him, and I suggest we talk to his family as well," replied the daughter, her face darkening under the shadow of a hovering gloom.

"Does he beat you, slap you?" asked the mother getting up in a jiffy.

"No, he does not, but he—"

"Then? What will we talk about?" Mother cut the girl short and stared at her sharply.

"But I am sick! I am sick of living in his jail. I am sick of his constant checks…. I am sick…really. He literally checks up on me every hour or so," replied the daughter with eyes full of tears as if clouds had given way to a gloomy weather.

"Try to look at things from a macro perspective. It is high time that you should become mature."

"Does merely slapping amount to cruelty? Even if he does not slap me now, he very well can, in future. I told you he has issues and they need to be resolved. I often tell him to visit a shrink, but the way he looks at me then is scary. I tell you, Mamma, he has issues. Imagine, he had guts to record my line-phone conversations. He even enquired with our neighbors about me!" added the daughter, clutching her mother's arm tightly, as if begging her to accept her pleas.

"Oh! Really? And how did you get to know all this?" asked the mother mockingly, pushing her away slightly.

"Of course, neighbors themselves told me in a hushed tone, and moreover, the way they give me those strange and sometimes sympathetic stares is appalling. I found the recorder under the table. Sometimes, he locks himself up in the room and refuses to come out for hours. It is too much…isn't it, Papa?" the daughter said.

"Understand the root. He loves you. Moreover, every boy shows his love in a different manner," the mother said, trying to pacify her.

"Being so obsessive and insecure only shows your own troubles and never a healthy love for anyone. Could this be love? He does not allow me even to work, only because he thinks I might start an affair with a co-worker or even divorce him to marry someone else. I had to leave a well-paying job under this pressure," the daughter said, taking a few small but hopeful steps towards her father, who was sitting in a corner, brooding over something.

"You had better not forget you are enjoying the comforts you could once only dream of. Life is short; do not waste these precious fun-filled years in such petty broodings, and I suggest you should try extending your family now. Have a kid or two and he will be set straight. It happens; boys do become mature overnight when responsibility falls upon their shoulders," said the mother, trying to throw in some positives.

"Family? Is freedom nothing, Mummy? Precious things have blinded you to my deep agony. Foreign travel can never be a surety of a happy marriage. He now avoids taking me out on social occasions, so how can you expect he will take care of his kids when he is not in his right mind? If he does not trust me, it is better to go our own ways," the daughter said firmly, as if taking a stand against the push her mother had been giving her.

"I agree he is a bit over-possessive, but he is handsome and well settled too. He fulfills all your demands, he provides for you, but you…" the mother said pacing up and down the room.

"That is because I cannot provide for myself and it is only because of you. You call this a bit! The small dreams that a girl harbors and the ambitions she nurtures over the years always fade behind the glittery wedding to the rich groom. They lie dead under the flowery aisle that often leads to a golden prison. He comes home for lunch, usually unannounced, and gives me strange stares that match the shades of an internal agony and helpless doubt of a juvenile," the daughter said as she looked her mother in the eye.

"See, do not give us your philosophy. We neither have time nor patience to listen to your unending and mindless crap. It would be better for you if you become a bit mature and hold your married life together instead of creating troubles." The mother heaped herself on the chair, avoiding all eye contact.

"See, I cannot live with a retard like him. Firstly, you did everything in such a hurry that I could not get time to interact properly with him. I got to know his rotten mind only after marriage, and now I am paying for your mistake. Look… Papa, are you listening?" asked the daughter as she wiped another tear that silently trickled down her somber face.

"Enough! I think you should stop this nonsense now and focus on your personal life. There are many witches out there; many a trap lies open for such men to fall in them. What will you do if he gets interested in another woman? Where will you go then? Hold your life, girl; hold him fast before he slips away. After all, who finds such a prince so easily!" the mother thundered, as if trying to make her leave the house in a firm manner.

"All right, there is no hope I can see, so I am going back to that dark ditch," the daughter said, walking towards her car.

"Your cousins could only dream of such a luxury car, and here you are hell bent on giving your happy marriage a kick," said the mother, admiring the huge SUV parked like a knight in shining armor.

"Oh, God! Just look at this! Do you even need any more proof? I switched it off for just around… maybe some twenty-five minutes! By what standards can one call it a happy marriage, Mummy?" the daughter cried as she gaped at the screen in fear and irritation.

"Oh! Errr… Ah… Probably you are right. I think it is time to talk to him and his parents seriously and seek medical help," the father interrupted quickly, not allowing the mother to utter even a syllable more when he saw more than twenty missed calls and fifteen messages on her phone, demanding her whereabouts.

* * *

The Deal

Behind a shut door with curtains concealing even the single streak of daylight that fell on the marble floor, two men, one fat and the other a frail, bald man, were engrossed in a fervent discussion. "We agree that your name is flawless," said the fat man to the bald one, sitting exactly opposite to him on a circular teak table. The well-adorned room looked elegant, and a few paintings done in modern art imparted to the space a dash of style.

"Then?" asked the bald man curiously.

"There are some other conditions we wish to discuss," he replied.

"With utmost sincerity; after all this is not our first time," said the bald man with a genuine expression on his face.

"I know…I know; this is not the first time you are putting in this much capital,' interrupted the fat man, "but now some terms are different." He glanced at another one sitting between both of them, at one side, who, from his gold-rimmed glasses, peered and blinked slowly a few times, and without uttering a single word, scratched his beard contemplatively.

"You can tell them everything; you know quite well that we do not cheat," said the bald man, also looking at the bearded one, who did not speak even when an embarrassing moment of silence made the air heavy around them.

"Look; we have seen only one of the two locations, and we know only the gross investment, all right?" The fat man tapped the table to emphasize his point with his index finger, which appeared swollen by carrying the weight of a huge blue stone embedded in a thick gold ring.

"So, what are those new and hidden terms?" the bald man asked, covering up the anxiety rising in his bosom.

"None; everything will be settled beforehand; we do not want any squabble later," the bearded man interrupted. The room was now filled with certain uneasiness, and both sides slightly shifted in their chairs owing to it.

"See, you know the full account and the articles," said the bald man, leaning towards the fat one.

"Even then, we want the full break-up. There is a lot of fraud in dealings nowadays," he replied, drawing a long face and thumping the table with his heavy hand; he shifted his gaze discreetly at the bearded man, who was intently listening to every word uttered until then.

"Break-up will make the fund-allocation clear, and we will know the total figure in each compartment," he intruded, leaning towards the table.

"We have a reputation to swear by, sir, and you have been closely involved the last two times as well. Both the camps are happy with our transparent dealings," insisted the bald man while carefully trying to maintain a phony softness in his tone. "We also know that we offered the highest. We are willing to invest more than those three parties. Take our word, not a single issue will arise."

"That is why I have referred your name," came the reply.

"See, a person expects good returns on all his investments done over the years," said the fat one, loosening his watch that clutched his wrist tightly.

"Of course, and that's why we are sitting face to face, sir. Count us in!" jumped in the bald man, noticing the slight distress.

"So, you can consult the list that has been given to you. It has all the specifications for the planning, interiors, and the list of exact brands required," began the fat man, concealing a grin of victory on his face. "Also, there is a lot of topsy-turvy games that go on in the name of international brands, so we want you to source only the original ones for us free of defects and in the warranty period."

"All right, we will go though the list again," said the bald one, picking up a thin bunch of stapled papers.

"Unlike all others, we have added only a few more items, that too because of the latest trends," the fat man harped, making the lines of worry a bit more evident on the bald one's face. He looked at the bearded man, who had now bent on his chair comfortably, lightly drumming his thighs.

"The bazaar is on a swing, and for such a bargain, you cannot even count the number of associations that will line up the second you back out," the bearded man whispered, staring piercingly at the bald one.

"No...not at all! This pact is very much ours, and we will, as I told you, intimate you the entire breakup of the reserves," he replied firmly.

"And we wish the original papers also, and the funding process and the portion of debts that you will likely raise," the fat man barged in.

"Papers?" he asked curiously.

"Lot of con, you see. Sir, we know the very pulse! People repair old cars and present them as new," the fat man said, tightening the noose.

"Not in our case. Last two times...you were also involved at each step, and the events went really smoothly. Did you notice any 'fraud' or repaired cars?" cut in the bald man, who had begun to feel a slight abhorrence for the bearded one.

"I do not doubt your integrity at all, but yes, prevention is always better," he replied calmly and gave a discreet smile.

"Have you met the designers we selected?" asked the fat man. "The opening ceremony needs to be grand; we wish a celebrity dance and music by a popular DJ."

"Yes, we will pay the advance. A celebrity dance will upset the budget, but if you can squeeze in some other compartment then..." the bald man said, his eyes still fixed on the bundle of stapled papers.

"This is trending and is in vogue. Parties are ready to rope in celebrities; it gives the desired exposure and elevates the reputation. You should understand," the fat man remarked with a frown, trying to gauge things from the grimaced face across from him.

"We have made things crystal clear. Moreover, for the function, we will call in a dance troop. Do not worry; it will be very grand," the bald man gave instant assurance.

"Press coverage?" asked the bearded man after thinking for a moment.

"Done. Some Hindi dailies will be paid the advance," the bald man said confidently.

"Hindi…all right," brooded the fat one under his breath.

"Hindi dailies have more circulation and earlier, too, we booked only the Hindi ones," said the bald man, concealing the rising waves of resentment from showing.

"Hindi dailies are fine. Do not worry," assured the bearded man.

"A photo-shoot has to be arranged," the fat man demanded.

"That will be done," promised the bald one. "Is there anything else?"

"Real pearls," the fat replied acutely.

"What?"

"R-E-A-L pearls," he emphasized on each syllable.

"What for? Who will notice that?" The bald man was left shell-shocked.

"It will be remembered for a long time and will only do your reputation well," the fat man answered with a poker face.

"The budget has already been stretched beyond the set limit. Please reconsider," he appealed to both.

"In such deals, the budget always stretches," declared the bearded one.

"Sir, now this is unfair! You do seem to have hidden terms." The bald man looked him straight in the eye, making the fat one more serious. "Real pearls are not possible"

"It happens. We have been very patient, and after all, in the long run, who will derive joy from all these expenses?" The bald one received a question instead of a reply.

"We have camps lined up at our doorstep. Even the agents will do anything to crack this deal. It is because of your reputation and his reference only that you are here," the fat man retorted in a slightly intimidating tone. "Otherwise, I have two more in waiting, with very stretchable budgets."

"We will see," the bald one grumbled under his breath.

"Okay! So let's seal this deal!" the bearded man grinned, pulling their hands and enveloping them into a political handshake.

"Yes, done," said both and stood up to hug each other.

The bald man stood up to take a leave. The fat one, with a bit of difficulty, stood up too, holding his enormous paunch and wiping the moisture from his layered chin, where dollops of flesh hung like meat at a butcher's shop.

"So, I will contact you tomorrow after consulting my wife," said the bald man. "She will get an auspicious 'muhoorat' for the engagement ceremony."

"Make sure it is grand too, just like the wedding. After all, our son is educated and well-earning. You have hit a jackpot!"

"Yes, do not worry at all."

"He will open many factories in the future, and finally, who will enjoy all this splendid luxury? His daughter only…isn't it?" the fat man asked the bearded one, and then he shifted his gaze at the bald one, who was standing like a defeated gladiator.

"Yes, why not! That is why I brought you this party from the many available in the market," smirked the bearded man. "After all, you are my wife's favorite brother! How could I upset her!" He then guffawed at his own petty joke, patting the fat man's back. Both grinned for his sake.

"Trust me! His girl is very homely and religious; rather, I would call her Goddess *Lakshmi* herself! She will not only care for you...day and night...but within a year, you will be cuddling a grandson too!" The bearded man's words made avarice reflect as a twinkle in the fat man's eye.

The bald man and the bearded one took their leave hurriedly. Later, the fat man heaped himself on a divan and gave a call to his wife, informing her of the wonderful deal he had fixed, admiring himself for having managed to extract successfully from the other camp more than what was decided. He then e-mailed a photograph followed by an SMS to his son who threw a swift careless glance over it and returned to playing Rummy with his friends somewhere.

The bald man arrived home, and after gulping down two glasses of water, called for his wife. She came in and their two married daughters, each holding a toddler, followed. He gave them a photograph of a chubby boy dressed in a loose jacket, standing in the background of the lion-fountain of Singapore. They stared at it for a minute and then handed the same to the youngest daughter, awaiting the final results of her graduation, and she, for the first time, had a passive glimpse of the man she would soon be sent to spend her whole life with.

* * *

The Return Gift

I lean against the window, watching the slow drizzle outside, an annoying sight. Still, you can have a respite if you are indoors, but what to do when there is a cloudburst? It can sweep you away ruthlessly to unknown lands and make you feel helpless and hapless. You turn around and see only a void where once your entire world was.

Life can definitely be not very lovely when you lie on an empty bed, all alone, between crumpled sheets, burning like a cigarette. The heat gets hold of your thoughts and you cease to think, cease to breathe, and lie like a sea shell that the ruthless waves suddenly kick out of its habitat before they disappear back into the ocean where they belong, without even giving the poor lone thing another chance or a second look.

I look at the sheets, the misshapen, punched pillows, and the bottles, all testimonies to my own folly, or rather a warning that now I need to realize that I have a spine too. I look at the half-burning cigarette and its smoke that seemed to fill every nook and corner with something. The only nice thing is that it does not leave it empty. I know that it will linger for a few minutes and then fade off unless you light one more to keep the empty room filled with, again, something. How long does this damned cycle go on? With my eyes searching intently across the room, soaked in dead silence, I ponder blankly.

This typical smell makes me think, makes me contemplate over myself. The intermingled smell of tobacco and a particular perfume always lingers on my mind and almost consumes me. I stare blankly at the rose-shaped box beside me; it has a velvet cover and is sparkling with fake glittering beads. If not attached to the solid earth that nurtures it, sustains it, the rose will fade; always fade, no matter how beautifully it is presented. I look at the bottle of imported whiskey lying on the table and also two glasses, one of which I am holding while I give head-on collision to the topics I always run away from. The other glass will remain half-filled, till I do something about it.

I cross my legs and take a puff. Oh! What a relief! *Or an escape?* I keep asking myself again and again. Good riddance. Whatever I may call it, it is definitely taking me in one direction I have never been before. I close my eyes for a moment and see something familiar—I hear the sounds, the tip-tap of a keyboard, the humming of ACs, and the soft murmuring of the staff —all these seem well-known... all these I wish to forget.

It feels like yesterday. A hand clutched my shoulder softly. "Are you all right? Did you have lunch?" Words as soft as snowflakes would melt as soon as I would hear them, relishing every sound, every syllable. "You are different; you are the stuff my dreams are made of," he confessed one fine day, in his office room. I savored every bit, my tired eyes tried to absorb all the moist warmness. Love is like a drug; it can cure you, or make you sick if given in overdose. In my case, it did what it is usually not meant for—it started killing me slowly, and by the time I realized it, I was half-dead, not unlike the cigarette stub lying near me, still smoldering in its own fire.

We met in an organization where we worked together. I joined later, under him. He was to mentor me, guide me, which he did—straight to his bedroom. What more can a man in his late thirties desire from a single woman, only a few years younger than him? I look at the bed and get my answer. Ours was a relationship of mutual trust and secrecy, and also of the love he offered even without asking. His children, he disclosed, were in a hostel since his depressed wife was mostly on medication when she was not throwing a fit. After my divorce, I always looked at every man with a certain suspicion, but we all know that emotions have wings but no sense. They are just insane; they can take you anywhere. "You are capable of unlimited love; you are the love, my honey," he said, making my dry lips taste the rain of a smile for the first time in years. I wanted to get lost somewhere in this shower, wanted it never to stop and to flood my life, burning with agony and loneliness. He drenched me in love, changed me from the dirt into a pearl, which until then, had been all alone at the shore; I learned to crawl slowly, without asking the unconcerned waves to take me into those comfortable but very dark depths.

"Today also, she threw a fit. God, I want to commit suicide," he would say, resting his head on my shoulder almost every day. "I am sick. Would you miss me if I, say, hanged myself?" he asked me once with such a passion and intense eyes that I just choked and rushed to hug him like a creeper that has to hug a huge tree, for it is so used to coiling around him for support, never even bothering to realize whether it really needs to be that intimate. He took my head in his hands and said, "I would have loved to get a mother like you for my kids," and I just smiled. On such nights, I would dream of chasing the kids in vast green fields.

This went on for a short time. Later, I changed my company. His laments about the deteriorating mental condition of his wife and of the adverse environment in the hostel that was making his kids sick continued. "Let us get married," I said one day, not prepared for an adverse answer. After all, who is, after realizing such a similitude in thoughts, and nights after nights spent together? He turned his fervent gaze away and sipped a drink, and then looked at me. Staring down, he said slowly, "She will not give me away."

"In such cases, it comes easy," I replied hopefully.

"No," he said in a cool tone. "My wife is unwell. She is on medication." He put on his clothes and bid me a nice goodbye after a while.

"Hmm...okay...." I could not say anything else.

Today, after we rambled about this and that and spent wonderful old age in our fantasy, would-have-been world, his phone beeped. It was a message that I managed to read, "I'm lvng for gyno. Today's appntmnt. Do arrive on time. Honey rmembr we hve a date tday! Kisses luv."

"I need to rush! My wife, it seems, has thrown another fit," he said. His expressions were classic, and I sincerely believed he should join a drama school. Leaving his drink and cigarette unfinished, he put on his clothes, looked at me pensively for a moment, patted me on my cheek, and said, "I wanted to take you out on a shopping spree. Honey, we'll go later." Then, like a torrent that takes away your small nest in its swirl, he placed a velvet box containing a pair of pearl earrings in my palms, closing it with a sort of a political handshake, and rushed out the door.

Tears swelled up in my eyes. Something pierced me inside like a bullet. Sometimes, honesty can bleed you to death. I do not blame anyone—no one is to blame. A corroding feeling peels your heart layer by layer and you cry out in pain, but you realize that your cries are not being heard. You wither away like a shiny tool, left in bad weather to rust and be worthless. You start living in the past; your back is towards your future, and you see no hope in the present. Of these three, a painful past gives you the sole joy that you badly want now—the joy of intoxication, of losing yourself. You think of all the pieces of your life, and slowly and diligently, burning alone, put them together. Your days are consumed in arranging the pieces so as to get a nice conclusion every time, and even before you know it, you are hooked to this slow-killing psychotic drug. You are sucked inside this never-ending emotional game that you have started but are inevitably going to lose. You see the final picture that is as ugly as your present, and you start all over again and again. You burn yourself out in the process and your heart bleeds. Eventually, you reach a point where you do cease to feel the pain, misunderstanding it as emotional independence, when in reality you carry with you the ever-rotting bundle of sordid emotions always searching for a vent. Slowly, you become desperate and the pain overflows even at the smallest prick, and you find that you are the new object of gossip in your circles. All pairs of eyes, it seems, are searching something in you.

What else is this man capable of? I wondered. Drenched in my humiliation, I wanted to cry, but my own tears defied me. After shedding a few of them, I now lay on my bed, my mind running in a very different direction. I just got up and kicked the front door, still ajar, very hard.

Today, as if after decades, a new day is smiling at me and I am standing straight to embrace it. Today, I am not longing for the waves to take me to those murky depths. Instead, I have realized that I am a pearl; I am the new dawn. I am shining like a dew drop fresh from the heavens! Just some old accounts need a final settlement, and for that, I have selected a pair of expensive cufflinks and a pink heart-shaped card with *"Thank You"* written on it in bold letters. I came home and picked up my old ballpoint pen, not his gold nib one.

> *"Thank you! It was awesome! You are indeed a tiger,*
> *every girl's fantasy! I just wish your depressed wife could*
> *have realized your potential. Good luck for her recovery."*

I packed it nicely and couriered it to his place, making sure this wonderful return gift reached his place only on some weekday!

* * *

Life Goes On

Sitting all alone on a busy railway platform, even though I am seeped in melancholy, I am not hopeless about the coming years. I gaze at the people around me. Basically, I have nothing better to do, so focusing on other things helps me divert myself from my own problems. This never-ending hustle bustle does not leave the platform barren even for a moment; it just never stops. "Life goes on," I repeat to myself. But the more I ponder, the more I fail to understand why it is so difficult to make some people understand so simple a fact.

A young lad in tattered clothes parades a fractured hand and stops in front of me, asking for some alms. I shake my head in refusal, but he tries to persuade me again. I do the same and he walks away muttering things. A candy man stands alone in one corner, waiting for customers, while the one near him is overflowing with orders. *Such is the life*, I think; *one man's loss is another's gain*. What is humiliating for me might be a vent of emotions for Ankur. What is a serious marital issue for me is a usual spat for my family. But in the end, who will be the one to decide who is right, rather more right? Who will, or who can, judge who will have the upper hand is the question.

The weather is cool and pleasant, and I see a few young couples moving around, holding hands. I wonder whether all of them will board the train, or are they here just for some evening walk? I notice yet another couple with the boy bent on taking a load of all the stuff. I muse again; if the boy carries the entire load, does that mean he can make the girl do her share by making her listen to his useless crap, or maybe by scolding her for no reason, or maybe by torturing her with his never-ending silence that is both bitter and paralyzing? Ankur was carrying my expenses, all right, but does that give him a right to pester me with his annoying, never-ending questions and reprimand me for answering honestly? My head aches, and I start for the nearby coffeehouse, which, too, is brimming with activity. Luckily, after a little wait, I get a table and place my order to a frail child waiter who rushes to get it. I check my phone for calls, basically for calls from my mother, or probably from him who might have got my point by now.

I begin to contemplate life. Coming painfully out from a womb of honesty can prick like a thousand needles. It is as painful as a real birth. Did you say honesty is a virtue? Yes, it is indeed, but a virtue, like a medicine derived from poison, can be fatal if taken at a wrong time, in wrong doses. I just wish I had known this elemental fact before so that I could have prevented this odd situation where I am reaping the rewards of dealing honestly with a man who was too weak to handle it. Taking a few steps back in time, I recall the entire scene, staring plainly at the creaky ceiling fan with a long pole.

That day, on an afternoon in our bedroom, Ankur sat watching TV while I was busy with my Sudoku puzzles. It was evident that he was thinking about something else; his face was towards me, and his eyes were restlessly scanning the floor. He first lowered the volume, fiddled with the remote, and then switched off the TV, tossing the remote on the sofa a few feet away. I noticed his agitation only after it became a bit longer than usual, for he has always been a bit weak in controlling his emotions. He leaned towards me, took my hand into his, and started off on a trail of events that end here, on this platform.

He pulled the Sudoku book from my hand and started in a soft tone, a sweet tone, like that of a child who is asking for something, probably repeatedly. In short, I could feel the embarrassment quite well.

"Sonal…Sonal, do you love me?"

"What sort of a question is this?"

"Seriously, do you?"

"Now don't be like a teenage drama queen, Ankur. Obviously, yes; otherwise I would not be sitting here."

"So tell me one thing."

"Ask."

"Okay…do you miss me…. I mean really long for me when I am away?"

"Yes," I replied, and I resumed my puzzle, for I thought of this moment as yet another of his usual juvenile attempts to proclaim his importance in my life. He again pulled the book away and did the same thing that he did with the remote.

"Okay, so there is no guarantee of life as you know."

"What?"

"What if I… we do not… I mean, are not always together. I mean to say, Sonal, what… what if I… I die?" He said this with grave contemplating eyes, introducing a factor of seriousness into his husky, childlike tone that was clearly a proper misfit, like one combines a wedding gown with a pair of tennis shoes, or maybe when you wear a cheap plastic watch with an expensive business suit.

"Ankur, I am going to get myself a cup of tea. Do you also want one?"

This time, too, I forced myself not to speak those magical words I always wanted to say. He grabbed my arm and leaned his head against my shoulder, shifting a bit closer, and said again, "No, seriously."

"See, Ankur; you are not going anywhere."

"If I go, then?" he asked deeply, looking me in the eyes.

"Hmmm."

"Seriously."

"Ankur, I am leaving. There are many things to do."

"No, tell me. Seriously," he repeated like a broken record, or more like a child trapped in a very limited vocabulary.

"Now what sort of a question is it? Why are you always asking such hypothetical questions, 'What if this…? What if that…?'" I lamented loudly, hoping it would make him desist from spitting out his crap again.

Luckily, my phone rang, but he disconnected the call, which, needless to say, annoyed me even more. I again thought of saying those three words, but I restrained myself somehow.

"No, seriously." The child in him had become rather a migraine for me now. These kiddish games of asking and procrastinating went on for another few minutes till he grabbed my shoulders with both hands and demanded an answer to what was to him a question of life and death.

"No, seriously, tell me.... I want to know the real truth.... Really, what will you do?" he asked, shaking me by my shoulders as if I knew the secret door to heaven or about his mother's past love affairs. I freed myself from his strong grip and looked him in the eye.

"Seriously?"

"Yes. Seriously."

"Can you handle it?"

"Just tell me...the truth."

I took a deep breath and said, "Life goes on. Ankur, life is a wheel, and it does not wait for anyone. The world stops for none."

My words were not sufficient for his twisted brain; he asked me for the "final" answer.

"What do you mean, Sonal?"

"Okay. I will remarry. See, God forbid, but if such a thing happens, I will definitely mourn, but eventually, I will have to remarry because life is too long to live all alone and too short to waste mourning over events that are inevitable and also irreversible," I added.

An eerie silence followed and spread like a shroud over us, and his face became pale and loosened up a bit. He chewed his lower lip, staring at his hands, his fingers fiddling with his wedding ring. "Tell me, honestly; come on," he said again with hopeful eyes.

Now this was the last straw; being no longer able to bear his unresolved confusions, dating back to his early teenage years, and his ever-growing immaturity, I got up quickly and repeated the same words more clearly, or say, with a brutal honesty, for basically, that was what he was asking for. Now it was for him to decide how to handle it and live with it. He got up and locked himself in the bathroom, and I left the room in a huff. For the next month, his strange melancholy and sullenness made my life miserable. Finally, when I could not take any more of it, I left home in a jiffy and came straight to this platform, hoping to go somewhere I could enjoy some calm.

A small womb, no more than a few inches, can give birth to things of gigantic proportions. Similarly, a small thing, a truth, a moment of honesty, passion, or a secret can blow things into gigantic proportions. Putting himself into imaginary situations has always been his favorite pastime, and now it was fast acquiring the shape of a passion. I was very sure of what he longed to hear. He wanted me to cry, sob, and beg him not to say such things and that I would die after him or that my life would become a barren desert and I would leave this world, tired and thirsty. What I told him was not to upset him or to make him pay for bearing with his unending growing pains; rather, it was the very truth. What if one becomes a young widow? Should she bear all her life alone, clapping at the laurels of others, or start her life afresh, leaving the tragedy behind?

I return to the present swiftly and blink a few times to absorb the hustle bustle a bit deeply. I see a young couple sweetly debating over who should carry the luggage. The wife wants to pick up a few bags, but the husband, too confident of his might, orders her to enjoy the walk to the train. He starts talking and a dutiful wife listens, or probably, it is his way of making her contribute to the journey. Dumping all his thoughts on her, not bothering how she feels, he goes on. The wife stops arguing and follows the husband. Now, if he collapses before reaching the train, should the wife spend her life crying over his corpse?

I now look at my watch; it has been almost an hour I have been sitting here. I buy a bottle of flavored milk and start sipping it slowly. I think of my parents' house. I was not able to fathom earlier that my sister-in-law would plan all this for a room. I should have noticed it much earlier when she started decorating it with cartoon posters and plastic furniture in pastel shades. The last time I went there, I did notice some changes, like the curtains were different; they were in soft blue with ribbons printed all over. The new table-cum-drawer was in baby pink, and the old wooden stools were replaced with *sitting dices*. However, that time I had some fresh wounds and did not bother much about all that. This time, the decoration made her message loud and clear. She was the lady of the house, and it was her choice to manage the rooms, and this one, which was once mine, with a big window and a nice view, was already allotted to her twin girls. My widowed mother stared at me helplessly. Dependency is such a humiliating thing, and that day—rather that very minute—I had vowed not to let it enter my life.

I dump the bottle and try to bring myself out of the reverie. I notice a few young urchins ogling at me hungrily, a beggar hovering about my bench, and a few eyes looking steadily at me. I blame myself for sitting alone, especially when I am a girl—rather, putting it a bit immodestly, a pretty girl. What did I actually blame myself for? Sitting alone, or being a girl, or being a pretty girl? It is difficult to answer in a society where... the less said, the better. My options are very limited, like a noose that chokes your breath, bit by bit tightening itself, even when you wish you could just run away from the entire dilemma, from having to choose from this or that, in search of a freedom to stay somewhere in the grey, not losing your mind by making a choice between black and white. I feel sick at the very thought of returning to Ankur's private hell. I discard the idea of returning to my home from where I was politely kicked out. But I have to do something...

Women can claim the paternal property, but the time is not right to file that case. I need to tackle the issue of my homelessness at this point. I can contact two of my friends in this city. One of them is married with a newborn to keep her awake all the time. No, won't be suitable. My mind races faster than ever. My relatives might help me, but all of them are quite far away. At the end of every stay here or there, I know what advice I will be given, and I feel sick from considering it even now. I could go to a hotel, but for how long? I feel somewhat dizzy for a moment; it seems I need some water immediately; I search for my water bottle and take a few sips, slowly.

Evening is coming to a fast end, like sand in an hourglass, and the hustle bustle of the station has increased. Going back is now out of the question. I tell myself like a chant "No going back," and I think that I am out to create a new world where no emotional tangles will drown me in unwanted grief and misery. I have already gathered much unwanted attention. But I stay put, trying to think of a way out and hoping God will definitely lend me some help. I close my eyes and mutter a small prayer; then I open my purse to take out my handkerchief. Suddenly, something catches my attention: a green visiting card. I know this person very well; she is an old college friend and a very loving soul, too. I give her a call from my cell phone with my fingers crossed!

* * *

The Reunion

The party was buzzing with activity; the guests seemed to enjoy the wedding reception heartily. The dinner was fabulous, and Shilpa was to receive a pleasant surprise. She occupied a corner seat, the only one that was empty while her husband Tarun was busy discussing politics, news, and budgets with his friends at the other corner of the park. All of a sudden, she noticed a thin woman walking towards her with somewhat fast and excited steps, and as she came a bit closer, sweet and nostalgic smiles broke on their faces. She was Varuna, her best friend from college, and it had been about two decades since they had met. Shilpa stood up and immediately offered her a warm welcome. They stayed together most of the time and often went to ice cream parlors and local eateries to savor the street food, which both were crazy about. The memories came to her in a flash and life seemed like a quick slideshow of memories. Varuna hugged her tight, and they both broke into smiles.

"Shilpa, you have changed a lot, buddy!"

"But you are very much the same, Varuna," she said hugging her again.

"So what's going on? I left the country for higher education right after college. Heard you got married?" asked Varuna.

"Yes, my dear; I got married two years later. I wanted to study, but a good match arrived so...anyway, you tell me!"

"Okay, nice. So what is your husband?" Varuna casually enquired.

"He is a chartered accountant."

"That's great!"

"And you? Have you got married?"

"Not yet. I am still the very same! Even now, I am too focused on my career. Actually, I did not get time to get married and all. Was so busy in jobs and all," replied Varuna, her tone taking a serious turn.

Shilpa could not stop admiring Varuna's fabulous figure and her toned body. She felt like a village woman who had entered a high profile fashion store. She looked at Varuna's well manicured hands, tastefully bejeweled with diamonds, her sparkling sari, and her high-heeled sandals, in which she walked as if on a ramp.

"Where is your husband?" asked Varuna.

"He...he has not come.... He was busy."

"By the way, why don't you come sometime to my place?" Varuna said.

"Sure, where? Are you still putting up in Keerti Nagar?"

"No, Shilpa. I bought a new spacious flat in Panchsheel Park," Varuna said and handed her a card that Shilpa carefully placed in her small purse. Then the two ladies took leave of one another. The gracious hosts were bidding good bye to the guests, and as Varuna phoned her driver, she saw Shilpa getting into the car with a man. "Must be a carpool," she muttered to herself.

However, the meeting had a different effect on Shilpa, and for many days to come, she remained a bit restless. She constantly compared herself to a well-maintained Varuna who was far more suave and attractive. Her stylish gait and flawless skin made Shilpa a bit nervous for some reason. Something inside prevented her from telling Tarun about this chance reunion.

A few days later, she received a call from Varuna. "Shilpa, why don't you come over this weekend with your husband to my place for lunch?"

"Yes, sure; that will be fabulous," said Shilpa.

The date was fixed and the time as well. It was nearly a week away, so Shilpa did her best to counter her inferiority feeling that had captured her since the day of the wedding. She went to a good salon, not her local one, and spent a good amount on various packages available there. All she wanted was to look good and not let Varuna score points in looks. After all, Shilpa had her reasons. Her problem was Tarun. She often thought about many such attractive and single Varunas in Tarun's office and even wondered whether he was having an affair with any one of them. Shilpa looked at herself in the mirror and a faint smile of reassurance broke out, for she was somewhat changed for the better. Her skin glowed a bit and she looked more confident than before.

Finally, the D-day arrived, and even though Sundays were never so exciting for her, a somber feeling was slowly taking over Shilpa like a slow poison. After having a light breakfast, she reached Varuna's place around noon. As she climbed the stairs, her thoughts took a turn and she noticed various things around her. A posh apartment with unconcerned, uninterested neighbors, a fabulous Varuna living alone in a huge flat where no sounds would escape through the mahogany and glass doors and windows. She had already made various cobwebs in her mind, and her insecurity had only heightened during the week. On Thursday night, casually, she had enquired about the MNC Varuna worked in, and to her not so pleasant surprise, came to know from Tarun that he had some great friends and clients there. This had given her a strange tension. Shilpa climbed the stairs and stood facing a beautiful, carved wooden door with Varuna's nameplate on it. With a somewhat uneasy feeling, she pressed the call bell. The door was promptly opened by a maid, dressed in a uniform.

"Maid in a uniform? Trying to be snobbish," mumbled Shilpa as she sat on a spacious sofa, admiring the tastefully decorated house, done in an Arabian theme. The decorative hookah in the corner gave the hall an old but classy appeal. The glass cupboards stood erect, as if proudly displaying their delicate bone china crockery. Huge canvasses, filled with modern art that Shilpa could not derive any meaning from, gave the hall a very tasteful appeal. She got a bit nervous, but in a moment, composed herself, and as a balm, reminded herself that, after all, a home is made by a homemaker and not a servant. She could never allow Tarun and the kid to have food from outside. She also reminded herself proudly of all the duties of a good housewife that she had performed over the years. She knew this feeling that made her uneasy was baseless. Neither Varuna seemed interested in Tarun, nor did he know who Varuna was. But fate could turn the tables anytime, she feared. She imagined Tarun and Varuna making out on their bed and closed her heavily done-up eyes in disgust. Suddenly, a soft slap on her back broke her strayed imagination, and she saw Varuna standing beside her. She was dressed in a knee-length blue dress and looked nowhere near her real age. Shilpa stood up and handed her the nosegay with a not so real smile, and they sat down to chat for a while till her maid set the dinner table.

The dinner comprised of a good seafood fare and reflected the dexterity involved in preparation.

"So did you like it?" asked her visibly elated hostess.

"Amazing, my dear," replied Shilpa genuinely.

"So tell me more about your family."

"We are a very small family, just my son, my husband, and me. Son is in a boarding school in Nainital and in-laws are in their ancestral town. They could not adjust with the fast-paced life of Delhi," she replied.

"So how come you didn't plan a second child?" Varuna asked, pulling a bean bag near to Shilpa's sofa.

"No, buddy, not now. Tarun keeps very busy," Shilpa replied in a bit melancholic tone. "By the way, he also says he doesn't want me to suffer labor pains again. You know, he is really possessive about me," Shilpa added, stressing almost every word.

"That's amazing!"

"Yeah. You tell me about yourself. Why you did not get married?" Shilpa asked in a casual but interrogating tone.

"Nothing, just after college I wanted to study further. Got admission into an American B school, and after that, did job stints at various companies. I shifted to India only three years back from Michigan. And yes, I am happily single," Varuna chuckled.

The gossip went on for a few more hours. After many heart-to-heart talks about college crushes, professors, and other sundry things, it was decided that Varuna would come for lunch at Shilpa's place on her birthday next Saturday. Shilpa took her leave and went home happy, but with a thousand questions and doubts popping up in her mind.

Meanwhile, she started weaving a thousand webs in her mind about how Varuna might seduce Tarun and why he would become interested in her.

"Varuna is attractive and not a plain Jane like me."

"She is suave and single."

Shilpa slowly melted in the heat of her own doubts. She looked at herself in the life-size mirror and felt like running away at once. Her once shiny flawless skin had become a bit wrinkled, and a few pimples could be spotted too. After the birth of her son, she had acquired much fat all over, that still lingered on even after a lot of workouts. She could easily spot white strands as well. All this made her feel like she stood low compared to a model like Varuna, who if she desired, could woo any man bored with his long wedlock in two seconds. *But why would Varuna do that?* Shilpa asked herself, staring helplessly at her disfigured torso. *Because Tarun is what Varuna is, good looking, suave and probably bored? One day, Varuna will displace me from my own home.* Shilpa was at once reminded of a lady she knew whose husband fell in love with a lovely Anglo-Indian girl. The affair made that man so smitten that he divorced his wife of twenty-three years. History can repeat itself. She reminded herself "Prevention is better than cure."

For the whole week, she tried to ask Tarun about the multinational company Varuna worked in. After all, both might have bumped into one another, started up a fiery affair, and chalked out a scheme to kick Shilpa out of her own house. However, she again accused herself of indulging in useless thinking and covered the mirror.

The birthday came on a happy note. Tarun gifted her a pearl and diamond necklace, and she received good wishes from other family members as well. Later, around noon, Varuna arrived in her chauffeur-driven car. Her hair was loosely done in a pony tail, and small diamond-like beads shone on her white silk kurta. Shilpa's heart skipped a beat, but she quickly reminded herself of her own expensive sari she had bought last week. Shilpa had tried to send Tarun out for sundry works, but he had refused and took to his pending work instead. When Varuna arrived, Shilpa greeted her warmly but all alone. Tarun was nowhere in sight. They both sat, and Varuna was surprised that no other guests were invited. After some light tea and snacks, the maid set the table for them.

"Where is your husband, dear?" Varuna asked innocently. That did not go down too well with Shilpa, but she had to call Tarun anyway.

"I'll just call him. Actually, the basic problem with him is that he is not at all social and hates going out. I always have to nudge him to go to social events."

"Ya, that's why you came to the reception alone too," said Varuna.

"Yes, I had to," said Shilpa with a forced smile.

After a few minutes, a casually dressed Tarun came down to the hall. Varuna was amazed. He was the same man she had seen with Shilpa that day get in the car. "Hello, Tarun!" Varuna stretched her hand out to him. After a few minutes, the talk diverted to their profession and companies, leaving Shilpa with nothing to say. She had always been a housewife and had never bothered to keep herself updated with current affairs or anything related to them. She felt as if she were the odd one who, in an instant, was kicked out of a group of intellectuals discussing things that would change the world in the times to come. However, more than that, she was bothered about her husband and her beautiful friend, who had potentially dangerous traits like her confidence, style, and on top of it all, her single status.

An English hit song was playing in the background. The maid was new and needed some supervision, so much to Shilpa's discomfort, she had to stay with her in the kitchen. Her constant peeping into the other room and the keen ear she was giving to their casual chat did not go unnoticed by Tarun and Varuna.

"You seem to be an introvert," said Varuna, trying to fathom him.

"Not really," Tarun replied. "In fact, last week, I got bored alone in the house when Shilpa went to a *satsang* at her aunt's place in Panchsheel Park."

"Satsang!"

"Yes. I dropped her there and had to pass time by myself."

Varuna's face acquired a shade of shock and anger. Last week, Shilpa was at her place and had said Tarun was always busy and now he had innocently spilled all the beans.

"I wanted to take her out this evening as well, but it is really nice that you paid us a visit," said Tarun in a jolly mood.

However, Varuna's mind was somewhere else. She understood the reason behind Shilpa's statement and the wedding reception where she had lied about Tarun. She was rather shocked at Shilpa's insecurity and felt a sense of pity for her degraded mind. She turned around and saw her holding the cake. They cut the cake in a plain mood. Both the ladies looked at each other in silence, and then an appalled Varuna left immediately on the pretext of an important client meeting.

* * *

The Bet

On a slightly chilly night in late October, an unhurried breeze that was careful enough not to wake the dull leaves cloaked the whole atmosphere in a stupor. Preeti, a woman in her mid-thirties, with a slender frame and wide, black eyes, craned her neck to get a view of the floor from her warm bed.

"It's time to sleep, Guddi," she said lovingly to her little daughter. As her pain still lingered, she had been prescribed a complete rest along with wholesome foods and regular medicines. The little girl, who was not much unlike her mother in looks, was very busy combing her doll. She now looked up, and dropping the comb and the doll, ran towards her mother and touched her belly. "Yes, my dear?" Preeti asked, turning to her side.

"*Mamma,* when is my sister coming?" the kid asked innocently.

"Soon, very soon!" replied Preeti, giving her a soft peck.

"Yes!" interjected Preeti's mother-in-law. "And very soon, we will have one more devil as if you were not enough. Millions of times I have told you not to refer to the baby as 'sister.' A 'brother' will be arriving very soon, a 'baby brother.' Got it? Now go," hissed the old woman, busy peeling carrots at the corner table, grudgingly. With her beak-like nose, button-like bulging eyes and thin grey hair, she seemed as ferocious as a hungry eagle out on hunt. Her sharp voice cut the soft silence ruthlessly. "Like mother, like daughter," she murmured under her breath.

"*Mummyji,* please, I know you are frustrated with me, but don't scold the child," Preeti hit back promptly, for no mother could bear her innocent child receiving an unfair dressing down. Guddi picked up her doll, and in fear, she hid behind a curtain, under the huge painting of Goddess *Durga,* and goggle-eyed, she stared at everyone, trying hard to make sense of the drama that unfolded almost every other day in the house.

"Oh yes, mademoiselle; now should I fall at your feet to apologize? As if the other one was not enough. She gave me twin girls and here both of you, mother and daughter, dying to add another name to the damned list," the old woman lamented.

"*Mummyji,* please, you kno—"

"*Arrey,* what *mummyji*? Your entire '*khandaan'* is like that; your mother could not beget any sons and now her daughter is here, repeating the history. Will your father pay us for their marriages and dowry?" The old woman spewed some more venom.

"Yes, Daddy will gladly pay. Okay," replied Preeti, trying to end the spat.

"Ha! Look! What a joke! He, who sent his girl with a fistful of coins, will pay for these girls, too! If only we had known about your family... *hai,* Bimla, you will be a slimy lizard for ten lives, I swear." The old woman began beating her bosom and cursed the matchmaker.

"What is your problem? What do you want? All this cursing and swearing will one day take a toll on me!" Preeti shouted.

"Look, look at the way she is talking to me. This is her tone when she has borne a girl. Only God knows how she will behave when she'll have a son," the old woman lamented, slapping her forehead repeatedly. She then stopped peeling the carrots and focused solely on the argument.

"Please, speak slowly, will you? Guddi is around. What will she learn from all this?" Preeti said in a whispering tone with a tint of request.

"Whatever. Remember that Gupta, the one in the corner house, whose nephew married that *Cheeni*? Their daughter-in-law has twin sons; how lucky they are, and that's why they're always happy," the old woman hissed.

"Is it? Then their daughter-in-law is still working too; they have not made her leave her job and sit at home. And, by the way, that girl is from Mizoram. She is a proper Indian *mummyji*," Preeti promptly corrected the old woman.

"Yes, yes, same thing; you just want to flaunt your knowledge all day. Anyway, if we let you work, is there any guarantee that you will have twin boys?" The old woman drew a long face.

"That's what! There is no guarantee. It all depends upon the type of.... Are you getting me?" Preeti looked straight into her cold and unfeeling eyes. "No one can take a guarantee in such things," she added, trying her best to explain rationally.

"*Hey, Ram*! Shut up, you shameless one. Think before you speak and, look at Mohan; she is now trying to blame you," she cried, waving her hands, and got up.

"Both of you please stop this. I don't want all this howling and all." Suddenly, Dr. Mohan intervened as he stopped checking answer sheets and sat down holding a cigarette between his thin lips.

"All right. Good night," Preeti said, jumping upon the opportunity and lying supine, pulled up the blanket. But the old woman would not give her an easy respite. "See this." She came near her bed and flaunted a gold bangle. "I got this after my third son was born; it was given by my mother-in-law. Understand?" she said proudly.

"So? Is this a race or what?" Preeti confronted her.

"I mean, we had to earn these, these prized pieces—not like you girls who just shed two tears and blackmail their husbands into buying all such fine jewelery. Another one is still with me. I would love to give you both once you give me a grandson. Am I asking much? I just wish you to get that test done," the old woman said in the manner of striking a golden deal.

"I can't believe this! You people...you take such things in this manner...earn and all. And the baby is doing fine, the doctor told me last week only. Are you not someone's daughter?" Preeti now sat up on her bed, considerably annoyed.

"*You people*... huh," she mocked Preeti, making wavy hand gestures. "I tell you, the second daughter will be a burden. Mohan, just go for the test. Where is the problem?" The old woman tried to involve her son, who got busy again, checking answer sheets.

Preeti rebelled "I have a problem. And I tell you now that I'll pray for another daughter only, for we are not superstitious and old-fashioned, less-educated ones like y—"

"Basically, you are just a headache for us. Just get the test done, and that's it," shouted the old woman, thumping the table in disgust.

"But we really don't wish to. You can ask your own son. I bet!" Preeti now sat up on the bed and challenged her, and received a strange stare.

"Yes, let's see who wins."

"Mohan, dear, just tell *mummyji* that you are against that test and fine with another daughter," she said ringing with optimism and confidence.

The women stared at him for a few moments in anticipation… with gaze still glued to the floor, he lit another cigarette and left.

The old woman chuckled nodding her head as Preeti's sobs echoed in the blank silence of the smoke filled room…

* * *

Charity

That day, her hall, tastefully decorated in Moroccan theme, was the hotspot of some serious topic. Glittering ladies with their bejeweled hands made quick gestures to support their revolutionary ideas. On the spacious imported sofa sat Mrs. Kumar, the hostess, and beside her sat four of her friends enjoying their fortnightly kitty party to the hilt. However, the only difference was that today they had decided to do the society a great favor by taking up the topic and idea of raising funds for unfortunate children.

Heavily decked in an embroidered suit, Mrs. Ansari started off, "My Sarah is so much into charity that even in school she would often donate her old clothes and shoes to servants' children. They literally worship her," she claimed, her green eyes dancing behind the gold-rimmed glasses.

"Yes, my Sonu too, still donates his old things to these people," Mrs. Khurana added quickly, fearing lest she should be left behind in the race for charity.

"But these people do not understand; they only want more and more...these people are never satisfied," added Mrs. Kumar, contemplating deeply, making a profound statement.

Mrs. Joshi's phone interrupted the serious debate for a few minutes. Her face flushed with certain happiness, but she made a point that she talked only in monosyllables that set the eyes and tongues rolling. Mrs. Khurana whispered quickly to Mrs. Ansari, "Did you get this?"

"Yes, open secret," she chuckled. "Must be her masseur from the salon!" she said and both ladies chuckled.

"Who was that, Mrs. Joshi?" asked Mrs. Kumar in a peculiar tone, as if checking to see whether her facts were correct. "You seem to be very elated!"

"Oh! A friend."

"From the salon?" asked Mrs. Singh, who had been quietly observing all this from the corner of her eagle sharp eye.

"You know, these masseurs, not all of them are good enough," she replied.

"That's why you have not left him yet!" interrupted Mrs. Singh, winking her good eye. The other one was of imported glass but looked quite real.

"Yes! I tell you, he is only seventeen, but the way his fingers move... amazing!" she said, closing her eyes and throwing her neck backwards.

"He must be good at other things also! We wish we had such luck!" replied Mrs. Kumar quickly, and once again, the hall ringed with loud giggles.

"And there is no issue as well, for I know, I know, what my man does on business trips...it is just like a tit-for-tat!" she exclaimed with a proud demeanor.

Meanwhile, between the hollow talks about appropriate tit-for-tats, Mrs. Khurana got a wonderful idea. She insisted they try to get the donation thing published in a local magazine along with their photographs. The idea was well-received, and they decided to donate good sums to get their photos published in the city's most popular magazine. Mrs. Khurana said she had some contacts and could manage the thing with ease. She immediately assumed an air of importance much to the irritation of Mrs. Ansari, who basically resented the fact that she wore an almost similar dress, spoiling her mood.

The kitty party progressed with full swing, and after the usual gossip about whose daughter was seeing whom and whose husband was spotted in Dubai's most notorious bar and the like, the lunch hour arrived. The kebabs were loved most of all amongst all of the items prepared by Mrs. Kumar's new maid. She was called in by Mrs. Ansari, who gave her a small tip happily for delighting her. The girl came and quietly collected the amount and went back to her work.

"Quite decent she is," commented Mrs. Singh.

"Yes, these teenage girls are easier to train and handle too. Her aunt will return from her village next month. And I tell you, that woman is a real headache," added the hostess, while using the antique silver finger bowl.

"My maid too is very good at cooking. I don't need to supervise her every now and then, and guess what! She even knows Italian cooking and Mishka loves pastas and pizzas," said Mrs. Joshi, stretching her arms and reclining into the sofa.

"By the way, what is Mishka doing these days? I had heard she was to do her high school from Shimla?" asked Mrs. Singh, turning towards her.

"We are still thinking over it," she replied, and quickly changed the topic to Mrs. Singh's teenage son and his recent spat with a notorious pimp at a rave party. Both the ladies exchanged sharp, cold vibes and waited for their chance to pounce upon the other with their prickly verbal swords. For a few minutes, a quiet spread in the hall, making the ladies discreetly notice each other's reaction to derive conclusions from them later.

Meanwhile, Mrs. Kumar called her maid once again and ordered her to take a plateful of kebabs to her brother's room upstairs.

"He just loves them," she laughed.

"He has just returned from a tour of Europe and is here for business. He is about to open a mineral water factory in the suburbs," she said proudly, as if it would be the only source of water in some drought-prone area.

The teenage maid, with a solemn expression, kept staring at the floor for a few minutes. Her face suddenly acquired a pallid hue as she filled the plates with kebabs. After a moment of silence, she said, "I will ask Munna to go," and left reluctantly.

"Why? Are you hard of hearing, girl, or low in wits? Why can't you go? Do as I say; I do not like useless arguing," the hostess thundered.

"Madam, I...I have other work in the kitchen," the girl muttered slowly, tossing the corner of her apron.

"Is my brother a hungry wolf? After all, who will pounce on a girl like you? Or do you think you are some fairy queen?" Mrs. Kumar said sternly. The girl stopped in between for a second and tried to wipe her eyes with the side of her crumpled sleeve that was quickly noticed by Mrs. Joshi. "Oh, man! These girls!" Mrs. Kumar shook her head, and then all of them proceeded with a board game. However, this kebab thing had set tongues wagging and eyes rolling till the card game engrossed the ladies.

At the end of the party, the donations were collected and Mrs. Khurana called her friend who worked for a magazine. "The bitch is asking for a bribe to put the story in the magazine, in the coming month's issue," she declared.

"Stuff her mouth with currency bills, but we must get some publicity," said Mrs. Singh firmly. She had always wanted to be a model, but an accident in a theme park had left her with only one good eye. She was now busy grooming her teenage daughter for various modeling and beauty contests that had actually taken a toll on the girl, who felt sick of constant workouts.

"Yes. Let us donate some more. If the kitty is big, the NGOs too help in marketing," said Mrs. Kumar again, displaying her wealth of worldly knowledge.

Finally, after much bargaining, the deal was set and it was decided that the pictures would be clicked at the office of the NGO that had collaborated with the magazine. After another round of Rummy, the ladies started to take leave one by one.

The first two days of the next week were full of excitement and anticipation. All the five ladies went to the NGO with their donation, a good sum by all standards, and made sure they looked their best. Mrs. Joshi spent a lot of time and money visiting the city's best salon while Mrs. Ansari got an imported facial done. Mrs. Singh chose the best garments to wear from her vast and somewhat unused collection, and the rest followed suit. After all, they were to be covered in the city's most popular magazine. The excitement was not subsiding, and until Sunday, it became difficult for the five women to hold it in. Finally, the much-awaited Sunday arrived. The ladies again met at Mrs. Kumar's house, each holding a copy of the magazine.

"You cannot even imagine how difficult it was for me to beat the stink of cheap phenyl," she said, twisting her small beak-like nose.

"Not easy for us as well," said Mrs. Ansari, reminding her that others too are not at home with such cheap stinks.

"These children rot, I say. No one bothers; one child even touched my cheek! Oh, God! What a dirty feeling it was!" added Mrs. Joshi in disgust.

"Yes, that's why I maintained a good distance," said Mrs. Singh, asserting herself with open palms.

"I did not even use the toilet; had to hold it till I got here," Mrs. Kumar cringed, slapping her thighs.

"But anyway, our photos have been published! I knew that greedy witch would charge for it, but finally, we have been covered in the press!" Mrs. Khurana cheered.

"This moment is indeed rare and deserves a celebration!" they shouted in unison.

The photos were carefully scanned and mailed across the world for all the jealous relatives to see. The party was celebrated again over the smoking kebabs, imported wine, and music, but the ladies, it seemed, were too busy to notice the young maid wiping her eyes as Munna served them pensively.

Lunch Boxes

The smoke and the heat used to pinch my eyes, but now, after three years of practice, it does not, and I can boast of a level of expertise at it that pleases my mother no end. Last week, when I made perfectly round chapattis, she even gave me an apple to eat that I am otherwise not allowed to touch! That was a wonderful feeling, but when I told this to my younger brother, he laughed at my face and the elder one did not bother. This hurt me. Anyway, I was telling you about the new swings the school has. The first one is like a round dish that goes round and round at full speed, and it feels like the earth is revolving because I know that the earth is round. The other one is shaped like a boat, in which more than two people can swing to and fro, and it is fun, too.

You know, I have a liking for white chalks, and when my father caught me eating a piece, I thought he would slap me, but he just went away unconcerned so, until a year back or so, I used to take a piece of chalk occasionally, like a guilty pleasure. I wish I could get colored chalks, but the school has only white ones, so I have to manage with them only. They come in really handy, such as when I go to the stream, behind the hummock; then I carry a piece to mark the trees so that even in the wee hours, I can find my way back home after attending nature's call. Sometimes, I just sit there after I am done with the morning rituals for a few minutes and draw on tree barks. My friend draws too and she says she draws better. She is such a jealous girl. Actually, I draw far better, and it used to be my favorite subject in school, but she just does not want to praise me. Still, I like her as she is my good friend and has even taught me an artistic type of stitching and embroidery pattern that her mother considers to be her strong point, and my mother, too, thinks it will come in handy a few years later when I will leave them.

I do not wish to leave this house, but she says, "What will you do here except eating and boring people to death with your blabber?" However, I do not think so, and I ask her to tell me how would she have perfectly round chapattis and a sparkling clean floor that shines like a mirror without me! Then she chuckles and mutters things like the slow rustling of leaves while chewing her tobacco, and says she will soon after get a daughter-in-law so I do not have to emphasize my importance like this. Mostly, she asks me to concentrate on making minimal wastage, like while cutting vegetables, I should extract the maximum out of the peels, and while transferring milk to this vessel or that, I should be sure that not even a single drop gets wasted; otherwise, my brothers will remain weak, and if they will be weak, they will not be able to protect me and take care of our family. This way, I take care that my brothers remain strong so that our family's name is carried forward.

One of the two lunch boxes in front of me reminds me of the dance function I took part in at school when I was five or six years of age. Each group member was given a plastic lunch box as a prize. I still feel possessive about it and want to use it too.

This morning when I went to the stream, I saw a few of my friends already sitting there, discussing how a pipe had burst in one of the toilets of the school and water entered one of the neighboring classrooms. It attracted so much curiosity that no classes were held for two days because the teachers were busy discussing the issue of the burst pipe. To make matters worse, the broken back gate wall had collapsed, making everyone feel unsafe, so for three days last week, we—I mean my brothers, me, and my friends—enjoyed playing around. I would get up early, finish all the work of cooking and sweeping, and then we would go outside and play till lunch. My mother says I should stay indoors in the evening because one of our upper-caste neighbor families has three tall boys who have come of age and often look at me discreetly. I could not understand a word, but as I am an obedient and good girl, I do what she asks me to.

One thing I could never understand is that despite the fact that I cook well and serve my father most lovingly, he never praises me or pats me like he does my brothers. I keep wondering what I should do to receive a hug from him. When I asked my elder brother about this, he said I should not fly or dream too high. My father, although he hardly speaks to me directly, too had said this once when my mother had announced that she was planning a visit to a famous astrologer with the birth-charts of my brothers. I was so excited upon knowing that he was a miracle man and could predict what would happen years from now, so I asked her to show him my birth-chart too, and then my father had all of a sudden roared slightly and said the very same words.

So, now that the chapattis have been done and the curry too is ready, I will quickly pack the two lunch boxes and fill up two plastic bottles with water so that my brothers are not late for school. After handing over the lunchboxes to them, it becomes difficult for me to wait till the late afternoon when they come back, for I so love to hear about the day's activities, like what they studied, what new things they did, which teacher joined or left, and all that. After all, I too studied at that same municipal school for a full five years till class third. It remains the best time of my life, and to tell you honestly, I am actually dying to go there once again, but I fear another thrashing. I would tell you more when my brothers return, but now I must hand over the lunch boxes, and then I need to start with the mopping of the house and then wash the clothes. Maybe we will meet the next time when I get some break from nonstop chores that keep me occupied. Take care!

* * *

Local Vocabulary

The Revelation

Jijaji	Sister's husband
Sari	A popular Indian garment
Dupatta	A long fine cloth ladies wear round their neck

Swati's Marriage

Baaraat	Marriage party from groom's house

Birthday

Aunti*jee*	"Jee" (or Ji) is added as a mark of respect while addressing someone.

The Deal

Muhoorat	An auspicious time for performing important tasks
Lakshmi	The goddess of riches and prosperity in Hindu Religion

Life Goes On

Sitting dices	literally chairs shaped like gaming dice cubes.

The Reunion

Satsang	Communal meet for prayer and sermons

The Bet

Durga	The goddess of power and an evil slayer in Hindu religion
Khandaan	Household
Hai	An exclamation of curse and resentment
Cheeni	A local expression for Chinese
Hey Ram	Oh! Lord Ram (a Hindu God)

About the Author

Ankita Sharma is an author and entrepreneur based in Faridabad, India. She is passionate about writing, reading, and portrait sketching. Her sketch works have appeared on the cover pages of *Ruskin Bond's World* and *Philosophical Musings for Meaningful Life: An Analysis of K.V. Dominic's Poems*. Ankita is also the author of *The Wedding Trousseau and Other Short Stories*.

You may follow her personal blog at *www.hummingwords.blogspot.in*

www.ingramcontent.com/pod-product-compliance
Lightning Source LLC
Chambersburg PA
CBHW050916120626

46552CB00004B/1602